BIKER'S PLUS SIZE LITTLE

Age Play DDlg Romance

Amanda King

ISBN: 9798839475250
Imprint: Independently published

1st edition

Cover design by: Amanda King

CONTENTS

CHAPTER 1

Brenda

I didn't even want to think about work, walking through the door and leaving the establishment behind me. It was a café.

For the most part, the place was nice, with elegant, long tables – small ones, too -, respectful customers, and the rest of the establishment was always clean and tidy.

The person charged with keeping the place clean always did a good job, sometimes to his own detriment. He was a nice guy and I really liked talking to him, but I just didn't see myself working in that establishment for long, after all.

I just didn't want to be working there for more than a couple of years, to be more precise.

Still, with rent, inflation, food prices, and the like, saving up money was difficult, though. At least I had an apartment and it was good enough for what I needed, and for the most part, it was also quiet.

When I first moved in, the thing I was most worried about was living under an upstairs neighbor that liked blasting music. It hadn't been the case so far.

In fact, the upstairs neighbor was actually a nice old man. He always greeted me when we saw each other, the rare times that happened, and I always reminded myself that I had to be nice, too.

After all, the last thing I wanted was to create dissent where I lived, and that would never happen.

I shook my head, deciding not to think about that right now. The city also looked nice around this time of the day. The sun setting in the distance, the small houses – and also the big ones – the high rises, the people walking here and there, some walking their dogs, and the like. It all almost made me think that I was living in a movie.

It was so good to live in a small town like this one, and I would never hide that.

And yet, there was also something depressive about it. One of the things that always made me think that was seeing other people kissing or holding hands, and more often than not my eyes noticed people doing that.

I shook my head again, deciding not to think about that as well right now.

I was just happy that I was going back to my apartment and wouldn't have to see my family again. The day they found out that I was a Little, they shunned me, kicking me out of the house, which was big and spacious, and I actually loved living there, despite how toxic everyone there was.

Sometimes, it was a living hell, but… I didn't even want to be thinking about those things right now as well.

It was peaceful, even if it was also a little depressive.

One of the good things about living here and so close to work was the fact that it didn't take me more than a couple of minutes to reach the apartment building.

After a couple of blocks, I was finally crossing through the main front door and then I took the stairs up to the second floor, where my apartment was.

I closed the window as soon as I was inside, and everything happening outside was muted. I couldn't even hear the cars and the pedestrians in the streets, and that was excellent.

When I learned that I was going to be living on the second floor, the first thing I thought was that the noises from the streets were going to be bothering me, but that didn't turn out to be the case.

And the fact that everything was so quiet around me meant

that I could be myself without difficulty.

As soon as I was completely alone and could breathe normally, the next thing I did was rush over to my bedroom. I threw open the door and stepped inside, looking around and finding a smile on my face even though it was brief.

It was good that I had my own place, but the best thing about this was that I could keep this side of me hidden, and I wouldn't have it any other way.

My bedroom was the most special thing about this apartment, and just being inside of it, I could already feel the nice smell that was in here.

It was so nice that it allowed me to close my eyes and focus on it, but even that wasn't enough – at least not enough to shut my mind to the fact that I was still single, and a virgin.

I really thought that by now that would have already changed, but it didn't.

Again, I decided not to dwell on stray thoughts that always killed my mood.

I shut the door behind me and I took Mr. Joachim in my hands. Out of everyone I knew, he was the nicest! I fell onto my bed, holding him in my hands over me.

I started to shake him clockwise and counterclockwise, rubbing him on my face sometimes as I said things to him that didn't make sense – not even to me.

"What should we play with tonight?" I asked him, brushing off the thought that he was basically my only friend.

Talk about being a loner, I thought, shaking my head and then putting Mr. Joachim by my side. I did that gently, trying to think about what else I could do right now so that I didn't have to focus on the bad parts of my life – and there were so many of them.

And I decided to dress up. I remembered that tomorrow I wouldn't have to work, and thus that gave me enough time to do this without feeling like I wouldn't have enough time to fully enjoy it. So, that was exactly what I did.

It took me some time, but by the end of it, I was in front of the body-sized mirror and looking at my reflection. I looked just like

Ariel thanks to my ginger hair.

It was one of the few things about me that I still liked when it came to my family.

CHAPTER 2

Merigo

"I'm going to finish your coffee right away, sir," she said, turning around and moving over to the other side, behind the desk, where she started working, pressing some buttons, and I could already feel that nice coffee smell in the air.

When it came to making coffee, she really was good at it.

I wasn't going to hide it. I had a crush on her and I knew that was something that would never change. I knew that it was kind of... complicated. Brenda would never fall in love with me, and I was so certain about it that I always told myself to never make a move.

That was why the only thing I was doing right now was ogling her. She was plus size and had one of the best, most lust-inducing bodies in the world, and just looking at it, my cock was already hardening.

Control yourself, I thought to myself, just happy that we were almost fully alone in the café.

She was working behind the desk, and there was this short, funny guy cleaning around the other side of the establishment. I could hear the sound of his mop scrubbing on the wet floor, and he was gentle and slow doing that.

I truly wished we were alone so that I felt more comfortable talking to Brenda, I thought.

I didn't know if it was just something I was imagining, but it was like she was feeling a little uncomfortable right now. Maybe it was the fact that I was looking at her curvy body, in which case I had to look away right now, which I did.

But looking outside wasn't exactly something I wanted to be doing right now, either.

The smell of the coffee was nice, but the outside of the establishment was quite boring. There was never anything different and exciting happening in this city and now was no different.

I sighed, looking to the right when I heard her setting down the coffee. I picked it up and said, "Thank you. It smells pretty good, as always."

When she moved her hand away, she ended up swatting it against mine, making the coffee slip out of my hand, and wet her uniform, staining it.

I was startled.

I didn't know how that happened. One moment she was moving her hand away and then the next our hands collided, spilling coffee all over her shirt.

And it looked like a mess.

A mess that I had to fix unless it was already too late.

But the look in her eyes showed me that it wasn't yet. I ran around the front desk, stopping right in front of her. This wasn't something that I did often, but there was no way around it.

There was no way that I was going to leave Brenda to fix this by herself.

"I'm so sorry about what happened. I don't know what I was thinking," she said, trying to remove the stain with her hands, but of course it wasn't working.

She needed to get a new uniform, and that was why I needed to take her to the changing room right away. I put my hand on her shoulder and I led her there, looking behind me to make sure that curious guy wasn't looking this way or had noticed what happened.

He was still mopping the floor and it looked like that wasn't going to change anytime soon.

"You don't need to be sorry about anything. It was an accident." And I was hoping, by saying that, she was going to start to look better, and she did.

Perhaps it was something to do with my voice, but I couldn't know that for sure.

What I knew for sure was that we were finally alone, in a room, and we couldn't hear anything happening outside. Obviously though, she had to go outside soon to make sure that no client would show up and find out that nobody was tending to the front desk.

Brenda still looked like she didn't know what she should do with her hands. All she knew was that she couldn't go out to work like this. Her stained shirt would make her clients think that she was sloppy and didn't care about looking her best, which just wasn't true.

"Do you have a spare uniform?" I asked and she shook her head, much to my dismay. Really? She didn't have a single spare uniform?

Unbelievable. And here I thought that the man that owned this café was a good guy. He was being that cheap? I had to go and have a talk with him. That couldn't remain unchanged.

"You are serious about that, aren't you?"

She nodded, replying, "I'm not lying. My boss is a good guy, but there are certainly some things about him I wish were different."

"Alright," I said, putting my hand on my forehead and looking content that at least she wasn't looking as nervous as before anymore. "We need to close up for today."

She bulged her eyes. "What do you mean that we need to close up for today?" She asked, sounding shocked even though she was beginning to realize it was the only thing she could do. "I work here. My salary pays the rent, the food on my table, my clothes, and pretty much everything I need to continue living. I can't live without it."

Well, I sure as hell wasn't about to start an argument all of a sudden here.

I just grabbed her hand without saying anything else and then I took her out of there and onto the sidewalk, making sure that she was coming along without this being forced.

And I was happy that was the case. Brenda was actually coming with me and we were going to close up the café even though her coworker hadn't finished mopping the floor yet.

He was going to be livid, but that was okay.

CHAPTER 3

Brenda

I had to call my boss that night to tell him about what happened. I told him and I was very specific about this – I couldn't work there again without a spare uniform, something I should have thought about before that accident happened.

He was actually nicer about it than I thought he was going to be. He told me that he wasn't just going to buy me another uniform, but plenty of them.

I was happy that he was understanding about it, but that evening did end with something I thought would never happen.

The guy that proposed closing up the café for the day? He was a biker and there were rumors around saying that he was the boss of a mafia family, but that couldn't be.

He was actually nice and even though he had this dangerous vibe around him, he was always sweet with me.

He always made me feel something different about him, something that made me want to be with him for all of eternity, even though I was certain he wasn't a Daddy.

Tonight, I was back in my apartment. Back in my bedroom, which was also my playroom, and the only place where I felt comfortable.

The day that I had to close the café thanks to Merigo's crazy proposal I thought my boss was going to fire me. Thankfully, that didn't happen even though I was so nervous about it.

So much so that my closet was open and I could see, from where I was, the handful of uniforms in it.

It was a constant reminder that I actually had the attention of Merigo, something I never thought was the case until that singular moment.

He was thinking about me, even at this moment, wasn't he? I asked myself, knowing that the answer to that was obvious.

I turned around slowly, finding Mr. Joachim by my side, and he was looking at me.

I had no idea what he was thinking, if anything, but he was actually looking at me, and that smile on his face was so comforting.

It was like it didn't matter what happened, everything was going to be fine.

I brushed my hand on his right cheek and then I picked him up, holding him in my hands over me.

"Mr. Joachim, you wouldn't happen to know what Mr. Pugliesi is thinking, right?" I asked him, but of course he didn't reply.

He was my Teddy bear and basically my only friend – at least the one that I felt comfortable with when talking about this - but he couldn't speak, something that I wished I could change.

I sighed, putting him back down on the bed, by my side. I was staring at the ceiling and didn't know what to do.

When I came home, I always felt so comfortable and so pumped up to be my true self, but I couldn't be that right now.

I couldn't be that because I just couldn't stop thinking about Merigo. He was so stunning. His voice was incredibly deep, his muscles were thick, firm, and he was also so much taller than me.

I could just imagine myself in his arms, his hands on my shoulders, his chin on top of my head, and him murmuring into my right ear that everything was going to be fine.

The truth was that I had a crush on him and I knew that it would never fade away.

The worst thing about this was the fact that he lived here and would never go anywhere. I didn't know what he was thinking, coming to live in a place like this.

Even though he was a biker and he preferred to make other people think that he wasn't well-off, I was certain that wasn't the case.

After all, someone that owned a bike like him had to have a lot of money.

I shook my head, sitting up on the bed. After doing that, I could already feel a little better and my mind was less obsessed with Merigo.

I didn't even know what I was thinking. It wasn't like he would eventually show up in front of my apartment building even though he said he was going to come.

That night, when we were arguing over what happened, we ended up exchanging phone numbers, and I also... told him that I had never ridden a motorcycle, and now he was going to show me what I was missing.

What an asshole, I thought to myself, cursing under my breath, thinking that I was going to fall for something like that.

He really thought that was going to happen? That even if he showed up tonight, I would jump off the bed and rush downstairs to see him?

If he thought that, then he was delusional, I thought, shaking my head.

I was going to dress up again tonight. I was going to pretend that I was Ariel and all the bad thoughts plaguing my mind would be over.

Everything was going to be fine and then-

A honk sounded just outside of the apartment building, and I knew that it was a motorcycle's honk and that it was also much like the sound that only Merigo's motorcycle could make.

I rushed over to the window and found him. He really was sitting on his motorcycle outside, and he wasn't wearing a helmet.

I had no idea what he was thinking, riding on his motorcycle without a helmet. He could hurt himself doing that, and why... was I even worried about that?

So assured of himself, I thought, but I still put on new clothes, sprayed some perfume, and then headed out in record time.

Even though I didn't want to admit it, the truth was that I was extremely excited about riding a motorcycle for the first time in my life. Not to mention that I kept on thinking we were going out on a date, even though he said this wasn't it.

Merigo made it pretty clear there was nothing unusual about this. Just him and me, riding on his motorcycle, having a little bit of fun, and then taking me back to my apartment, and we weren't even planning on meeting up more often so that we could do this again.

Apparently, his life was boring.

I would never have thought that was the case.

CHAPTER 4

Merigo

"Hi there," she said, looking so happy right now it was impossible to put it into words. She was indeed coming with me. I thought she wasn't going to after I honked outside of her apartment building, but she did and now she was standing right here with me.

I patted the backseat of the motorcycle with my hand, inviting her to sit on it. She did after swinging her leg over the motorcycle and putting her arms around me.

When her arms were around me, I already felt so much better than before.

I felt like my life was actually meant to be doing this and not to be leading the Pugliesi family, something that I had been avoiding this whole time.

It wasn't that I didn't like the people under my command, but that I just didn't want to be bothered with all the administrative things that came with being the Dom of the family.

Adelmo and Curzio left after finding their partners, and here I was, wondering if I would ever also find a Little.

I didn't think that was possible, especially when I liked living here and I couldn't see myself moving out to find a new home.

It was such a small city that it was almost like a village.

There just weren't enough people here so that Littles existed. They all lived in the big cities, and I was certain that was where I would find my other half.

I shook my head, deciding not to think about those things. Brenda was with her arms around me and her head was almost touching mine. I could feel the warmth of her body and it was so great that I felt like I was protecting her.

I turned the handlebars, making the motorcycle roar to life. Then, we took off and were cruising across the city slowly.

It was her first time riding on a motorcycle and I wanted to make sure that she was enjoying it.

I could see the wind blowing her hair behind her head, and I didn't know if it was because I was going too fast, but she tightened her arms around me.

And I could see myself doing this several more times in the future. Now that I had her number and we were beginning to bond, I could see myself going out on many more dates with her, and yet… I'd already told her that this wasn't about that.

Well, I wondered for how much longer I would be able to keep up that lie.

We rode out of the city and found ourselves on a hill overlooking it.

Seeing the city from up here was incredible and always breathtaking.

Brenda didn't have the habit of exploring the city, so I knew that this was her first time seeing it from up here.

We could see everything from this point.

The view was more than breathtaking. It was the kind of experience that Brenda would never forget, and I was certain about that, seeing the way that her eyes were looking at the city, turning left and right, and taking everything in.

"I told you that you were missing a lot," I said, telling myself this – it didn't matter what happened now, I was always going to keep her protected and even though my second-in-command wanted me back in the big city, it would never happen.

I was already doing something different and much more rewarding here and I just didn't want to go anywhere.

My hand looked for hers, and I grabbed it.

She didn't protest, and it just felt natural to be holding her hand like this.

I thought she wouldn't, but she did and she looked up, and I could see that connection forming between us becoming stronger.

Was this moment going to develop into something bigger? I didn't know, but we were saying so many things now through this stare. I supposed that she had already grown a little tired of marveling over the city, and now she wanted to say a couple of things to me.

"We shouldn't be doing this," she said.

"Why not?"

"I shouldn't be letting this happen."

"Let what happen? You are killing me now with anticipation, and it's making my heart tight just thinking about it."

She bit her bottom lip, looking away, but that wasn't going to cut it. I wasn't going to have it. I put my hand on her chin and then I lifted her head so that her eyes were looking at me again.

"Even though we never spoke much before this, I already knew so much about you."

"How come you already knew so much about me?" I never thought that she paid me much attention. I thought that, to her, I was just another client that came to the café for some coffee.

I thought that was everything I was to her.

She squirmed a little, holding her hands together in front of her. She was so cute trying to protect herself like that.

And she was acting so much like a Little and was so submissive as well that the only thing I wanted to be doing right now was to protect her, and out here I could do that without difficulty.

CHAPTER 5

Brenda

I was still standing on top of the hill and he was still in front of me, looking at me with curious eyes.

I knew what was going on in his mind and I had no idea what I was thinking when I spewed out the truth.

I thought it was something that I would keep to myself for the rest of my life, but now everything was coming out, and I couldn't control it anymore.

The truth was that my life was boring and when I didn't have much to do, I spied on him. Well, not really like in the usual, more common sense of the word, but I always asked people that lived in the city about him, and they were always so receptive to my questions.

They always said that they didn't know much about Merigo, other than the fact that he was a biker and Italian.

Quite an interesting combination, and one that made me feel some heat between my legs, too.

I had always had a thing for Italians, bikers, tough and rough men, and he fitted the bill perfectly.

The only problem was that I knew nothing would ever happen between us. Nothing until this singular moment that he was with me, where we were on this hill overlooking the city at night, and it was so romantic that I could just imagine him kissing me.

"The truth is that I had always had a crush on you," I finally blurted out, and I felt like it took everything I had to do that.

It was the most difficult thing I ever said in my life, and I didn't know how to deal with it anymore.

I knew that when I looked up, I would see his eyes looking at me and him wondering what the hell was even happening. He was probably thinking now that I was going mad or something like that, and then he would leave me in front of my apartment building and would never see me again.

That was my fear, but when I looked up, I noticed that he wasn't looking at me with judging eyes.

It was much more different from that. He was looking at me with comforting, gentle eyes, and he even put his hand on my cheek, as though that was his way to show me that he also had been thinking the same thing this whole time.

"I thought you would never say," he said and it shocked me.

I never thought that Merigo would confirm to me that he felt the same way. So, all those times when I thought he was ogling me, when he was looking at my behind when I had my back turned to him, and pretty much every other similar moment… It all meant that he also wanted me?

Thinking that, I felt like my mind was going to explode, and my knees were weak all of a sudden.

He put himself closer to me, and his hand was still on my cheek. I had no idea what he was thinking, but he was dipping his head, making me think that we were going to kiss.

Was this really going to happen? So suddenly? We didn't even know each other properly yet. We didn't even know each other's families, and he was going to kiss me, just like this?

Just thinking about it, my heart was speeding up and there was nothing I could do about it.

Our lips connected and I felt fireworks exploding in my mind. I thought I was going to pass out, but he was holding me to him, and his hands were the only thing supporting me right now.

He was so much bigger than me that I felt protected, cared for, loved, and so many other things at the same time. And the kiss… It was the best thing that happened today, and I knew that the competition wasn't fierce, but still… I would never forget it.

His lips were incredibly sweet and he was kissing me passionately. He wasn't using his tongue – not yet, anyway – but I could feel his lips rubbing on mine, slowly before he picked up the pace.

And I could feel his saliva on my lips, the warmth of his body, the hardness of the muscles of his chest, and how he made me feel loved even though I always thought I would never find anyone.

I wondered what he was thinking, finding out that this was the first time I was kissing someone.

Even if he didn't like it, he certainly wasn't letting that get in the way of his enjoyment of this kiss.

Breathing was becoming more difficult and my body was starting to get sweaty, and yet he was still treating this like it was the most normal thing in the world to him.

And when Merigo pulled his head back, he was looking at me with kind, comforting eyes.

"What just happened?" I asked, not understanding any of this. One moment I was riding with him on his motorcycle, the next he took me to this hill overlooking the city, and now he was kissing me. Huh?

When did everything happen and when did it change so suddenly? I asked myself, suddenly realizing that he would never be able to learn who I really was.

He would never know that I was a Little. Even if he thought I was hot and that there was a connection between us deeper than our kiss, the moment he found out that I liked toys for children, games, pretending that Mr. Joachim was alive and that he was my best and only friend would be the moment when he would kick me out of his life.

And just thinking about that happening was making me fear for my future.

That was why I pushed myself away from him, turning around while hugging myself.

He lifted his hand as he tried to reach out for me, but it didn't work. I was beyond saving. I didn't think that tonight was going to hurt me so much, but the truth was that I could already feel a tear coming out and rolling down my cheek.

I was a Little and felt so ashamed of myself.

It was a side of my life that he should never, would ever find out about, and I promised myself that things would happen that way.

CHAPTER 6

Merigo

I was in my house, lying on my bed and looking at the ceiling, thinking about Brenda. She left me like that without saying anything, and I didn't have the strength to ask her what happened.

But I knew what happened, or at least I thought I knew. I kissed her before the time was right. I ended up doing that because I thought it was the right thing to do at the time, but now I realized that I was so incredibly wrong about it.

We didn't know each other well, but I felt this deep connection to her and I thought that she felt the same way.

But I figured that the first thought that crossed her mind was that I was taking advantage of her. She must've thought that. It had been her first kiss, I could tell.

She was incredibly clumsy when kissing me. I didn't think that it was anything that ruined it, but obviously, she probably thought differently.

I just wished that I could call her and tell her that it wasn't what I thought, but I would feel so uncomfortable doing that.

I knew I was supposed to take the next step, but how was I going to do that when she obviously didn't want anything else to do with me.

I knew she didn't because the next thing she said after she walked away from me after our kiss was that she wanted me to take her back to her apartment, and I did that.

I did that without uttering a complaint about it, even though the ride back to her apartment building was empty and lifeless.

I felt like something deep was missing in me and that I would never recover it.

I shook my head, deciding to sit up on the bed and then get off of it.

I was back on my feet on the floor and feeling better. And what could make me feel slightly better than I was feeling right now? It was getting on my motorcycle, and as soon as that thought crossed my mind, it was the next thing I decided to do.

I put on my jacket, pants, boots, and everything else, and then I hopped on my motorcycle. I turned on the engine and I let it run for as long as I thought it was needed so that I felt better.

There were very few things in life better than feeling and hearing the rumbling of the motorcycle's engine underneath me.

But obviously, there was something better than that, and that was feeling the arms of Brenda around me, her warmth behind me, hearing her breathing, and a couple of other things I would never forget.

I wasn't going to leave the city no matter what happened, and my routine meant that I would eventually end up seeing her in the café again.

After sitting on my motorcycle, I took a stroll in the city, eventually reaching her apartment building. It had no more than 5 floors, and she lived on the second one.

Looking at it from the outside, I noticed that she had pulled close all the curtains, and they were thick and heavy, blocking all light from the outside. I couldn't see the inside of her apartment at all, something that tempted me.

I mean, I would never break inside it, but I wondered what her apartment looked like. I couldn't help but think that was where she kept all of her secrets, including that she might be a Little.

I would never straight up ask her if she was. I still thought that we had a chance. I thought that she would eventually call me, saying that she didn't mean anything, that she felt something strong for me, but yeah... Nothing of that would ever happen, right?

That's what I thought, stepping away from there and reaching the only pub in the city. The first thing I thought would happen here was me finding Brenda in this place too, but scanning the interior, I couldn't find her anywhere.

Thank goodness, I thought. It wasn't that I didn't want to see her ever again, but that I thought it would be too awkward, and I just didn't want to be feeling even more down than I was right now.

I sat down with one of my friends here in the city and we knocked back a few drinks. Nothing really out of the ordinary, and he did notice that something was wrong with me.

I thought that he was going to ask me what that was, but he didn't, something that actually made me feel more comfortable around him.

He did give me a tip even though he probably didn't intend to. I walked out of the pub thinking that I should probably do something – anything – to make Brenda realize that there was no ill will between us.

I didn't know if that would work, but I could still try, right?

I was back in my house, back in my bedroom, looking at the ceiling and realizing that I felt better. Not better to the point of making me forget everything that happened, but better overall, and thinking how much I wanted to make my possible solution to this problem happen.

Something that could make Brenda think that there was no animosity between us...

I sighed, thinking about that and turning around after taking off my clothes. I lied down in my bed and was ready to sleep, but then I remembered that I forgot that I had to take my clothes off.

After I did that, I was finally – and this time I meant it – ready to sleep. I closed my eyes and fell asleep, but even while I was sleeping, I was still thinking about Brenda.

She was becoming an obsession, and I didn't know how to deal with that.

I never felt obsessed with anyone before.

CHAPTER 7

Brenda

Working today was a thorn in my side. I didn't want to work, but I still had to. After all, after that incident with the coffee wetting my uniform and having to call the boss and ask him for spare uniforms, I had to be diligent and punctual about my work, and I would never risk losing it.

And yet, I still felt so empty, especially after finding out that Merigo didn't want to see me again.

I knew that because he never came back to the café for his usual coffee, and we didn't talk since then. He didn't call me, didn't try to reach out, and in other words tried to pretend that I didn't exist.

Just thinking that, I couldn't help but start to hate him, and even the things that I usually did to help pass the time... I didn't find enjoyment in them anymore.

Would that eventually change? I didn't know, but I wasn't in the mood to be thinking about that sort of thing right now.

I just had so many problems in my life, my family included. They called me sometimes, trying to pretend that they still cared about me, even though I knew that wasn't the case.

I didn't know what they were thinking, calling me to talk to me, but those were always moments when their words came in from one ear and went out through the other.

I shook my head, brushing those thoughts out of my mind.

I was walking outside on the sidewalk, noticing that this was very reminiscent of that day when I thought there was something deep happening between me and Merigo.

I knew that he wanted me, but then I realized that he could never find out I was a Little.

I was so embarrassed about it that the next thing I did was walk away from him and decide that I would never talk to him again, even if he showed up in the café.

I supposed I should be thankful he never did, I thought, minutes later finally reaching my apartment building.

I looked at my apartment on the second floor, and I dreaded opening the front door.

I didn't want to be reminded that there was this side of me I could never change. I was a Little. I liked playing with my toys, dressing up as princess Ariel, talking childishly with Mr. Joachim, and coloring my coloring books.

I liked doing all those things, and I wanted so much to have a Daddy that would say there was nothing wrong with me.

I opened the front door and I plopped down on the couch, looking at the TV and realizing that I didn't even want to watch anything at the moment.

Was there even anything I could watch that would wash away the terrible thoughts in my mind? I didn't think so. That's what I was thinking, eventually realizing that when I crossed through the door, I didn't notice the small box by the entrance.

It was pink and it was wrapped in gift paper, and it even had a tied lace that I could pull. It was cute and exactly what I wanted. It made me feel better already.

So how the hell did I not even notice the box when I entered the apartment? I asked myself, realizing how stupid I was. And without giving it another thought, I just stood up and headed over to the door.

I opened it and I found the box sitting by the entrance. So, I wasn't crazy or imagining things when I remembered there was this box by the entrance of my apartment.

I decided to check the sides of the box to see if there was

anything on it that showed me who it was from, but there was nothing. Whoever had sent it to me didn't want me to find out right away who he or she was, and I was curious why that was.

It made me curious about this and it also helped me not dwell over the terrible things going on in my life. I really didn't want to fall in love with anyone.

The last time that happened, even though nothing came out of it and it certainly didn't reach the same proportions as what happened between me and Merigo, it left me absolutely devastated.

That was why I didn't want more of that same shit in my life.

I closed the door behind me and started to open the box. First, I pulled the lace and then ripped the gift paper, and after that, I set the box down on the table in the kitchen.

I pulled open the top part of it and I took a step back, gasping when my eyes landed on what was inside.

For a moment, I really thought that I was going to find a severed head in there. Perhaps someone wanted to play a trick on me, had found out about my Little side, and was going to try to destroy me and drive me out of the city.

But it was actually something a little different from that, and I was thankful for that.

It was just a bracelet. It was made of gold, and I knew that it wasn't fake. I knew that just by looking at it, even though I was no expert at that sort of thing.

I just knew that it was expensive, and whoever had bought it for me… And who was that? I didn't know, but there was a small piece of paper just under the bracelet.

It was also a different kind of bracelet. It was more suitable as a gift for Littles like me, I noticed.

The bracelet had a small Ariel head attachment on it, and I knew that when I put it on with the rest of my Ariel outfit, it would make it look even better! I would look even more like the Disney princess, and I was overjoyed, thinking about that.

And then I started to read what was on the piece of paper, and I couldn't hold back the smile that appeared on my face.

I just never thought that he would do something like this for me.

CHAPTER 8

Merigo

I was sitting on my motorcycle and waiting for Brenda to show up. Was she going to? I didn't know, but I was hopeful. I didn't even know what she was probably thinking now after finding the box by the entrance of her apartment.

When she opened it, she would probably think there was something deeply wrong with me.

After all, she was an adult and the gift I gave her was more suited for kids. Little girls, in other words.

I didn't think that she would even open the curtains so that she could see I was outside.

I was outside and waiting for her to do that so that I could finally go up there and talk to her in person about everything that happened.

I would tell her I was sorry that things happened the way they did.

I shouldn't have kissed her while assuming she wanted that to happen.

I was gripping the handlebars of the motorcycle, and it was like time was passing in slow motion around me.

As usual, nothing was happening in the city and everything was so quiet the only things I could hear were my own breathing and the wind flowing around me.

I didn't know if she was a Little or not, but I ended up talking to the guy that worked with her in the café, and he told me how much she liked Ariel, and I thought that was the perfect opportunity for me to give her something she would never forget.

A small bracelet for a gift.

I was sure that it was going to bring a smile to her face, and I just wanted that to be a turning point in her life for the better.

That was why I was so anxious right now, waiting for her to open the curtains.

But time was passing and that wasn't happening. I was beginning to grow anxious, and not even sitting on my motorcycle was helping me with that.

I sighed, looking away and deciding that I wasted my time coming here.

She wasn't going to open the curtains, wasn't going to come down, and would never even talk to me again.

I supposed that my second-in-command was right when he said I needed to go back to the big city and take control of the Fiorentini family again.

They wanted and needed me, after all.

I turned on the engine of my motorcycle and I was going to do just that, packing my bags and everything I took here when I suddenly heard the window on the second-floor opening.

For a moment, I thought I was imagining things, but then I realized that wasn't the case.

The sound did indeed come from the window on the second floor, and it was opening and the person that was behind it was none other than Brenda. But the most striking thing about this wasn't even that she did that.

Actually, it was something else.

Now I was beginning to understand why it took her so long to open the window and show herself.

She had dressed up. She looked just like princess Ariel, and she was stunning.

The first thought that crossed my mind was that she really was a Little, and I didn't know how to react to that. Should I go and straight-up ask her if she was? I didn't know, but I was already getting off my motorcycle.

She turned around and disappeared into the living room, showing up a couple of seconds later outside of the apartment building after she threw open the front door.

I never thought that she would be so happy she would forget she didn't want anyone to see her dressed as Ariel, or maybe I was only imagining things.

Perhaps I was making assumptions that weren't true at all.

Either way, I was just so overjoyed that I couldn't stop smiling.

She rushed over to me, arms wide and spread out. She held me tightly, rubbing her head on my chest and saying over and over, "I don't know why you gave me the bracelet, but I'm so happy you did. This whole time, I've always been thinking about how I could make my Ariel outfit look better, and I never thought that I was missing this. I thought that there was nothing wrong with it. I thought that it was already complete, and yet I always kept thinking something was missing."

I didn't know exactly what she was talking about, but I was just happy that she was feeling incredible levels of joy. I was actually beyond happy that she was feeling more complete thanks to my little gift.

She looked up after taking a step back. After all, it wasn't like we were girlfriend and boyfriend – not yet, anyway.

And then she took my hand and started to take me to her apartment building. Wait, was this really happening? Was she actually going to take me inside her apartment?

I didn't know, but I was just so fucking glad that this was happening.

And she looked like she was going to reveal everything to me. When she showed up dressed in her princess Ariel outfit, I knew something was up, and I wanted to find out everything about it.

And if she was a Little, I would tell her I was a Daddy.

CHAPTER 9

Brenda

When I realized the mistake I made, it was already too late and I was already outside of the building and holding his hand as I led him inside it. But perhaps the most striking thing about that wasn't my sudden lack of awareness.

Perhaps it was the fact that he was actually coming along and wasn't stepping away from me as quickly as his legs could take him.

It was the opposite of that, and even though he wasn't the kind of man that smiled often, he was smiling right now.

It was faint and almost imperceptible, but it was there on his face, and I just couldn't stop looking at it.

Now, it was already too late and I told him I was going to take him inside my apartment. We were already going up the stairs, and then we were in front of the door of my apartment.

This was still so surreal, I thought.

What the hell was I thinking? That I was really falling in love with a biker? I didn't know, but at this time, there was no point in trying to stop anything anymore.

I opened the door and we stepped inside my apartment, and I shut the door just as quickly, but without making too much noise. I just didn't want my upstairs neighbor to be bothered by anything I did.

Merigo put his hand in front of me, stopping me. "Care to tell me what the hell is happening here?" He asked, putting his hands on his waist as he showed me that he was confused about this and slightly disappointed in me, too.

After all, I wasn't behaving well. I was being naughty and doing things so wrong he would have to punish me as if he were a Daddy.

I bit my bottom lip. This was difficult and it would be a decision I would never be able to back away from, but there was no point in hiding the truth anymore.

"I think there's something about me you need to know," I confessed, looking into his eyes and hoping that he was going to be understanding. And even though he was a biker, there was something about Merigo that always told me he was understanding. He was very open-minded. "And I want you to promise me that you won't hate me for it."

His eyes changed and he looked more nervous about this. Perhaps he was going to say that he was concerned about what I was thinking and what was going on in my mind, but he kept his lips sealed. He was actually waiting for me to say my next words.

But this was actually better done differently. I grabbed his hand again and took him to my bedroom. It was just as I had left it. It had Mr. Joachim, the letters on the wall with my name, everything looking pinkish and childish, and even some scribblings on small pieces of paper showing how much I wanted a crib even though, here in my apartment, there wasn't much space for it.

I opened the door and he stepped inside, his eyes going wide. The first thing I thought he was going to say was that he thought there was something deeply wrong with me, and if he said something like that, I would be so disappointed that I would start to cry.

And time was passing and he wasn't saying anything, making me feel so curious about what was going on in his mind. I knew that he was impressed by what his eyes were witnessing, but he was silent, and that was the worst thing that could be happening right now.

"Well?" I asked, hoping that he was going to say it actually looked cute or something of the sort.

"This whole time, I've been suspecting that you were a little," he said, looking down at me.

I almost jumped where I was. Did he just say that he thought I was a Little this whole time? I didn't even know how to react or what to do with my hands.

I stepped away from him not because what he said bothered me, but because it was completely unexpected.

"And I'm a Daddy, too," he revealed, grabbing both of my hands this time and making me lock my eyes with him.

My eyes bulged and my heart skipped a beat. The last thing I thought he was going to say was that he was a Daddy, but now that I was thinking about it, it made sense.

I thought that he was going to say he felt there was something deeply wrong with me after seeing what my bedroom looked like, but he didn't do that, and now this was happening.

My heart was speeding up.

I didn't want to think that he felt something strong for me, but we kissed, he told me he was a Daddy, and all the requirements were met.

He could become my Daddy and make my life whole.

"Merigo…" I said, and saying his name was the only thing I could say right now, and that was okay.

"I think we should give ourselves a chance," he said, kissing my lips, sending shockwaves of pleasure in my body. It went tight.

I didn't know what to do, and he was all over me, kissing me, his hands exploring me, and this was the best moment of my life. His lips were as sweet and tender as I remembered them, and I didn't want this moment to end for anything.

That was why it felt like the kiss lasted for hours.

"I think the same, too."

And when I said that, I noticed how breathless I was.

Was this really going to happen? Was I finally going to have my first boyfriend and he was going to be my Daddy to boot? I didn't know, but everything was progressing quickly and it was impossible to be stopped.

All I knew was that I could give ourselves a chance.

CHAPTER 10

He said he was going to kiss me and that it was going to be amazing, and I couldn't help but wait impatiently for it.

He said he was going to kiss me again, and I just couldn't wait until that happened.

And one more thing that I couldn't wait until it happened was finding out how he looked without his biker vestments. I was sitting on the bed, and it was kind of strange. I was still dressed as princess Ariel and this was all happening the way I thought it would.

I always thought that my Daddy would be taking off his clothes right in front of me, and my heart was tight just waiting for this to finish.

I mean, I was waiting for him to properly start this.

And when he lifted up his shirt, I could finally see what his torso looked like without it, and it was breathtaking. Perfect muscles, perfect everything.

I could even see some sweat drops riveting down his skin, and I just wanted him to take me, to make me his, and I knew that he was going to do that.

He was slow as he took off his clothes, and then he let me watch him as he took off his pants and pair of boxer briefs, too, finally showing me how big his cock was.

It was so big that I didn't think he could fit it inside of me.

I checked his body from bottom to top, scrutinizing every little detail, and I could see that a pre-cum drop was already glistening at the slit. I couldn't help but feel like licking it, and I knew that he was thinking about letting me do that.

I took a deep breath in when he climbed onto the bed, covering my field of vision as he did that.

I couldn't even go anywhere. His arms were locking me where I was, and I wanted so much for him to penetrate me, but was he going to?

This was still just our second date, and I knew that doing that would be sudden. I didn't want to rush anything.

It was for that reason that breathing was becoming so difficult now, and I knew he knew that, too.

"You are my Little, and I want you to never forget that," he said, and his voice was so low and throaty.

His fingers started to explore my body, and he lifted my dress, exposing my sensitive parts for the delight of his eyes.

"Yes, Daddy, I'm your Little," I said after I took off my dress, and he finally had access to my entire body.

It took a little bit more time than I thought it was going to, but I was finally without my dress and pretty much every other thing that was covering my body before.

It was just like I said. His fingers could explore my entire body, and that was exactly what he was doing.

Merigo didn't hold back before he started to pinch my nipples, grazing his fingers on them.

He knew how he was doing that and how to hit every right spot, making me arch my back as I felt ripples of pleasure in my body.

"You are so lovely, my little one," he said right in front of my face, and I thought he was going to kiss me, but he didn't. If there was something that I was beginning to learn about Merigo, it was how much he liked to tease me, just like he was doing now.

I knew that we had just kissed, but I still wanted more of his lips, and I wished he could give me that right at this moment.

But he wasn't going to.

Without saying anything about it, he reached for his pants and pulled out a condom, showing it to me.

He put it on his cock, which was a bit disappointing, but I knew that I couldn't have my first time with someone I was still beginning to love. I knew how dangerous that would be, and I just didn't want to do anything I would regret later.

Even though I could see myself building a family, I wasn't going to do that – or at least I wasn't going to start that at this moment.

For now, my life was only about him and me and how happy we could be together.

After he put the condom on his cock, he pulled me to him, and then he entered me, stopping the moment when he found my hymen. When he did that, he looked into my eyes as though he was trying to read my mind.

I knew he didn't need my permission, but he was only going to take my virginity when I felt safe doing that, and now I did.

I told him that with my eyes, and then he thrust his hips forward slowly, making sure that he was stretching me while limiting the pain. He was so proficient doing that, and I noticed how good he was fucking me when he started to piston in and out of me.

Thus, it wasn't long until I started to match him thrust for thrust, and some minutes after that, I came. My body started to convulse and my eyes rolled inside my head.

It was the best fuck of my life and I knew that nothing would ever top it.

I could barely breathe.

He had to come at the same time as I did, and with that look in his eyes – it was obvious that he enjoyed it as much as I did.

He plopped down on my side, and then he put me between his arms, holding me tight to his hard, godlike body.

And before we fell asleep, he murmured into my ears how much he loved me and how much he was going to turn my life around.

We were finally going to move out of this city.

MERIGO'S EPILOGUE

I told her that we were going to move out, and I promised myself that I was going to do good on my word.

She was already putting everything in her suitcase. The good thing about her apartment was that she didn't have much she needed to take with her. And the other things that she couldn't take in her suitcase, she was going to order a transportation company to carry them for her.

In the meantime, I was already feeling a little impatient. Even though I liked the city, there was no denying that I had kind of grown tired of it, and I had been fantasizing about this moment for so long, even though I had always said to myself that wasn't exactly what I wanted.

I thought that all I had always wanted was spending some time here and away from the Fiorentini family, and now I realized how stupid that was.

When she turned around, I asked, "Do you want a little help with that?"

I noticed that she was having difficulty closing the suitcase.

I said that she didn't have a lot to take with her, but it wasn't completely true. Even though she didn't have as many things as I thought she did, she actually had some things that couldn't properly fit in the suitcase, and she needed a huge, spacious bag for them.

She looked at me, smiling broadly. Her smile was always so shiny and captivating. I didn't know what it was about her teeth, but they were always shiny, even when she was indoors.

She was going to enjoy living in a better place, I thought. Even though the city where we were going to was massive and quite overwhelming, she was going to enjoy having a better bedroom that at least had a window.

"Yes, Daddy," she said, nodding once and frantically, and then I walked over to the suitcase, closing it tightly, using most of my strength.

There was always something so rewarding about hearing her saying the word 'Daddy.' This whole time, I had always wondered what it would be like to hear it from my Little, and she was making that a reality for me.

I looked at her and noticed that she was blushing.

"You are so strong, Daddy," she said and then I took her hand. I didn't need to, but there was something special about taking her all the way down to where my motorcycle was.

I had asked her about it, and she was completely okay with my proposition. We were going to do a road trip to my new house in the new city where we were going to live.

She had said to me before that she was comfortable riding for that long on my motorcycle.

"I'm always strong for you, little one," I said and some seconds later we were finally on the sidewalk in front of the apartment building, where my motorcycle was waiting for us.

I climbed on it and she climbed behind me, wrapping her arms around me. She put her suitcase on the side of the motorcycle, where there was a support for it.

I turned the handlebars and the engine of the motorcycle roared to life. She tightened her arms around me, but I knew that she felt safer hearing and feeling the motorcycle.

I turned my head around and I said, "Don't worry – I don't like boasting about it, but I'm a fucking good biker."

"I trust you," she said, looking up and I took off.

It took hours, but eventually, we were in front of our new house, and I was tired. So much so that I just wanted to fall onto my bed, and I knew that Brenda thought the same way.

After all, even though she wasn't the one riding the

motorcycle, she still had to be with me during the entire trip.

When I looked behind my shoulder, she said, "I think that after this, I just want to be spending some days inside the house, being who I am and without having to go anywhere for anything."

I smiled, getting out of the motorcycle and helping her do the same. Her hand was so delicate and everything about her gave off the same vibe that I was always worried that anything I did could hurt her.

That was why I was always extremely careful whenever I had to hold her hand or touch her. Even when we had sex - and especially when that happened - I had to be so careful that it was odd.

In my line of work and in my job, being careful just wasn't something I was used to doing, and now was no different. But I didn't worry; as time passed, I was going to get better at that.

"I feel you," I said and then I took her to the house after getting the suitcase from the motorcycle. I opened the door and put my hand on her shoulder, pushing her forward slightly so that she stepped inside and felt more comfortable doing that.

"Well, it's so big," she said, pointing out the obvious.

Compared to her old apartment – and it felt so right to be saying this – it indeed had more space than we probably needed.

Just the living room was much bigger than anything she was used to, and I could only wonder how I thought that leaving my old house in that small city was something I was able to tolerate and even like.

But looking back at everything that happened, there was a purpose to it, and that was me finding the love of my life.

I just couldn't imagine myself living these days without her.

BRENDA'S EPILOGUE

I wasn't going to lie about it - I didn't think he would eventually go through with it. Merigo promised me that he was going to take me to see my family. When I said to him that I despised them, the first thing he said was that I needed to make peace with them.

And he was right about that.

Every time that I thought about my family, I felt a deep pain in my heart, and I knew that it would never heal as long as my situation wasn't resolved.

That was why we were standing outside of their house. My parents' house, to be more precise.

I was going to tell my entire family about my relationship with him and why I thought he was the best man for me.

He was holding my hand as though he wanted to protect me no matter what happened, and I was certain that was the case.

There was no way that this could be happening any differently, right? I was always feeling like this, everything making me feel so anxious, my heart so tight.

The truth was that seeing my parents again was so anxiety-inducing that I just didn't want to do it, and yet I knew I had to.

His hand holding mine was comforting, but still, I didn't know if it was enough.

It was difficult for me to even press the doorbell button, and I didn't know if I should do it.

I tilted my head up and noticed Daddy looking at me, his eyes comforting.

"I know you can do it. They should know that you are with me now," he said and even though I knew he was right about it, I still wanted to run away from this.

And yet, I still pressed the button by the side of the door. It rang the mechanism in the house. I thought I could then hear footsteps behind the door, but I was mistaken. They were actually coming from the side of the house.

I could see my father coming, and I also saw some wood dust and particles on his clothes, showing me that he was sawing something at the back.

Where was my mom? I didn't know, but I was certain that she had to be somewhere nearby, most likely inside the house.

His eyes were wide. He thought that I wasn't going to show up so suddenly and without warning him first about it.

Every time he could, he said that I always had to warn him about everything that I did. He was always controlling like that, and I was certain that was something about him that would never change.

He stepped toward me, and I could see from the way that he was walking that he was being extremely careful about this. If it was only me, he wouldn't be acting like that, but things were so different because I was with my Daddy.

He was by my side and I noticed him puffing out his chest so that he was more imposing than normal.

Even though my father wasn't someone that anyone wanted to mess around with, he knew that he wasn't the most dangerous man around and that he couldn't start saying shit to me without repercussions – not now that I wasn't alone.

"Who are you?" He asked, stopping when he was a couple of steps from us. "I don't know you. I'm happy that my daughter is here, but I really don't know you, and you better start explaining what's going on."

"Can we go inside?" I asked, and when I thought that he was going to start to shoot me several questions about this, he didn't. He didn't do that because someone just opened the door, and that was my mom.

She was also looking at us with wide eyes, and her reaction was completely normal.

She didn't think I would come here today and much less that I would be with a man as tall and as imposing as Merigo. Not to mention that he gave off this dangerous vibe and that she shouldn't say anything that could hurt me, even though she wanted to.

She cleared her throat, invited us inside the house, and then we sat down in the living room. My parents were across from me, and at least there was a coffee table between us, separating us.

My Daddy was by my side, and he was still holding my right hand. He was going to support me all the way through this, and it couldn't be any different.

Then, I started to explain everything. From the beginning. It took me a lot of effort and by the time I was done, I was breathless. I hadn't talked for so long in all of my life, and I felt like I just poured out everything I had.

"It's a lot to process," my father said, but he stood up and then held out his hand, offering it to Merigo. "But it looks like you really care about her, and even though there's so much to learn about you, I'm going to trust her with you." He took a deep breath and they shook hands. It was a strong, determined handshake, and I could almost see the sparkles coming from it. "And if you ever hurt her, I'll be the first to know."

Except that he wouldn't be, but that was okay. I wasn't planning on keeping in contact with my family after this. I was actually only doing this because I wanted to settle it. I couldn't keep living my life with my mind dwelling over how much my family wanted me.

It wasn't that I thought that was going to change now, but at least they knew what was going on in my life and that I was with Merigo.

Mom cleared her throat, stood up as well, and shook hands with Merigo. It was also an intense handshake, but when they retreated their hands, I felt so much better.

"I think the same thing that my husband just said."

And after we talked about a couple more things, we had lunch with my family. It was awkward, but then everything was finally over. I bid goodbye to my parents, promised them that I would be back - even though I probably would never be – and then I stood outside of the house with Merigo in front of me.

He put his hands on my waist and pulled me to him for a kiss, and it was a kiss I would never forget.

It meant so much to me.

The End

Leave your review. It really helps us authors!

TEASER: HIS PLUS SIZE LITTLE

Mafia Cupids - 1

The last thing I thought I was going to stumble on today was this menacing, frightening man that was lying on my bed. He was nothing short of jaw-dropping. Even though the clothes hid most of his body and he was unconscious, I could tell that he was those things and perhaps even much more than that.

He was just lying on my bed and even though I was helping him with his wounds, I had no idea what I was supposed to do right now. My hands were working. There was this hole in the side of his body, just under the rib cage, and even though it looked pretty bad, I knew that he was going to pull through.

To be honest, I was more frightened that he was going to wake up and find out how silly my room looked. The walls painted in pink, the stuffed toys spread around, and my teddy bear that was by the side of the bed – it also had something about a side of my life I always hid from other people, even the ones that considered me their friend.

I wiped the sweat that was on my forehead. I was a nurse – or at least I was going to be one again. They laid me off not too long ago and I was still living on the unemployment fund that they gave me. It was enough to pay the bills, but just barely so. My dingy little apartment was something that ashamed me, too.

Just looking at this hunk of a man lying on my bed, I was sure that he was someone used to richness and luxury, something that I never ever exposed myself to in my life. And yet, I was still going to keep helping him because, as a nurse, that's what I did.

Minutes later, I was finally finished patching up his wound. A lot of blood soaked the bedsheets and I could smell the blood in the air, but that was okay. It wasn't like I wasn't used to those things anyhow.

I was just so tired right now. This man was limping outside my bedroom when I noticed that he needed my help and that was when I went out of the room as quickly as possible. In a moment, I had found him still limping outside, and then he fell inside my room. I had gasped and it was a shock, but now not anymore.

I was already getting accustomed to the fact that this stranger, who was even carrying a gun with him, was in my apartment.

One other thing that was comforting me right now was the fact that he was still breathing, albeit slowly.

I couldn't help but wonder what he looked like without his clothes on. But that was a thought that I quickly brushed aside. There was no time to think about those things. It spoke about how lonely I always was, I thought, lamenting that part of my life.

Minutes later, when I was finally going to turn around on the little stool where I was sitting, I heard him grunting slightly and then he opened his eyes quickly. He found me and then he latched his hand on my wrist, something I thought he wasn't going to do.

After all, it was the first time that a patient was gripping my wrist so tightly after just waking up. His eyes were completely intense and glassy. He was looking at me with this intensity in his stare and I felt like he was going to kill me.

After all, even though he was slightly wounded, I was small and didn't know how to fight back against anyone. Even when a cockroach was hiding in the furniture and my eyes happened to catch sight of it, I always screamed at the top of my lungs like it was going to kill me.

Seconds later, though, the strange man eased his grip on my

wrist and he let his arm fall to the side of his body. He was still breathing slowly, and my heart rate was speeding up. He didn't say anything and it was infuriating. I didn't have to go out to help him and a thank you would be nice, I thought.

I turned around slowly so that my body was facing him. The man wasn't looking at me anymore, but rather at the ceiling and he was breathing slowly and carefully. I could see his chest expanding and contracting.

Moments later, when I was already opening my mouth so that we could begin to talk, he said, "Thank you for saving me. I would probably be dead right now if it wasn't for you."

I didn't even know what to say. I was so mad and so ready to dis him for not saying anything about my help, and now he just thanked me. I supposed that was why I was blushing and why he was chuckling when his eyes finally looked at me again.

But he didn't say anything about that, which was comforting and relieving.

"Well, I'm glad you are okay. I thought you were going to die," I said and then he didn't say anything else. There was this moment of silence between us, and it was awkward and I wanted to break it. "Are you going to tell me who you are?"

He stood up slowly, grimacing. It was obvious that the bullet wound still hurt him a lot and there wasn't much I could do about that, so he was just going to have to keep living with it for the time being. And me being the nurse I was, I had to do something he obviously didn't like.

So I put my hands on his shoulders and then I tried to make him lie down on the bed again, and he was already saying angrily, "Hey, I don't know what you think you're doing, but I'm okay. I feel better and I can stand up at least. Or if not that, I can sit on the bed."

"I'm not going to let you do that. I'm a nurse and I'm worried about you. You need to rest so that you can get better."

I was treating him like a child, but it was for a good reason. Even though there were so many mysteries surrounding his bullet wound, I was going to make sure that he was going to get out of my apartment feeling better and well.

He groaned slightly and was still strong enough to push back against my hands. I figured that this man was stubborn, but I didn't think it was this much and I also never thought he was still so strong. I mean, I was small and slightly chubby, but I thought I still had enough strength to push him back down.

When he was sitting on the bed, I just retreated my hands and then put them on my waist. I was shaking my head as I said, "I don't know what you think you are doing, but it's obviously not going to help you. I'm the nurse here and I'm the one that knows what I'm doing."

"I'm Adelmo Fiorentini, and it's good to meet you, nurse."

The way he said that made me blush. He was holding out his hand as if he truly cared that he was making my acquaintance. I didn't have another option but to give him my hand and I felt his fingers engulfing it like it was nothing. There was something about this man that gave me safety and pretty much everything else a Little like me could be looking for.

I knew that it didn't make sense, but what if he was a Daddy and was still single?

I shook that thought out of my mind right away. There was no point in believing in things that couldn't be.

His hand appeared to be holding mine for what felt like minutes, but when it was over, it was probably just a couple of seconds. His hand was particularly warm, big, and calloused.

It was the hand of a man that went through a lot before ending up where he was. His life was never easy, he was always facing the worst of things, and he had plenty of enemies.

Those were just some of my suppositions regarding his life and even though I knew that they were spot on, I wasn't going to just kick him out of the apartment. Not until he was feeling better. If I did something like that, I wouldn't feel okay with myself.

"And are you finally going to tell me your name?" He asked, raising his left eyebrow. Even though I didn't want to admit it, there was no denying that he was my type of man. There was just something about his face that made me want to kiss him, slide my hands on his cheeks, feel the bushiness of his beard, and do pretty much everything else I could.

Nevertheless, those things weren't going to happen right now. I was single and I was going to remain so for a long time.

I took a deep breath in and said, "I'm Dessie. Dessie Johnson."

SIMILAR BOOKS

SERIES - BIG ME

MM ABDL. Lots of age play, sweetness, peppered with steamy scenes, and sprinkled with age gap dynamics.

1. Pampering Little Miguel
2. Endless Crayons
3. Teaching Little Jerry

Or download all of these books in this bundle:

Sweet Holidays

ABOUT THE AUTHOR

Amanda King writes sweet ABDL, age play romances. Packaged with steamy scenes, her books are fast-paced and, more often than not, they deeply explore the world of age gap relationships.

When she isn't writing, she's reading for inspiration. Some of her most popular stories are "Pampering Little Miguel" and "Endless Crayons."

www.ingramcontent.com/pod-product-compliance
Lightning Source LLC
Chambersburg PA
CBHW071451150726
48000CB00006B/2521